THE
MAN WHO
PLANTED
TREES

THE
MAN WHO
PLANTED
TREES

JEAN GIONO

Wood Engravings by Michael McCurdy

Afterword by Norma L. Goodrich

CHELSEA GREEN PUBLISHING COMPANY
Chelsea, Vermont 05038

Originally published in *Vogue* under the title

"The Man Who Planted Hope and Grew Happiness"

Copyright © 1954 (renewed in 1982) by

The Condé Nast Publications, Inc.

* * *

Library of Congress Cataloging in Publication Data

Giono, Jean 1895-1970

The man who planted trees

I. Title.

PQ2613.I57H5813   1985   843'.912   85-9925

ISBN 0-930031-06-7 (alk. paper)

Printed on recycled paper

FOR a human character to reveal truly exceptional qualities, one must have the good fortune to be able to observe its performance over many years. If this performance is devoid of all egoism, if its guiding motive is unparalleled generosity, if it is absolutely certain that there is no thought of recompense and that, in addition, it has left its visible mark upon the earth, then there can be no mistake.

About forty years ago I was taking a long trip on foot over mountain heights quite unknown to tourists, in that ancient region where the Alps thrust down into Provence. All this, at the time I embarked upon my long walk through these deserted regions, was barren and colorless land. Nothing grew there but wild lavender.

I was crossing the area at its widest point, and after three days' walking, found myself in the midst of unparalleled desolation. I camped near the vestiges of an abandoned village. I had run out of water the day before, and had to find some. These clustered houses, although in ruins, like an old wasps' nest, suggested that there must once have been a spring or well here. There was indeed a spring, but it was dry. The five or six houses, roofless, gnawed by wind and rain, the tiny chapel with its crumbling steeple, stood about like the houses and chapels in living villages, but all life had vanished.

It was a fine June day, brilliant with sunlight, but over this unsheltered land, high in the sky, the wind blew with unendurable ferocity. It growled over the carcasses of the houses like a lion disturbed at its meal. I had to move my camp.

After five hours' walking I had still not found water and there was nothing to give me any hope of finding any. All about me was the same dryness, the same coarse grasses. I thought I glimpsed in the distance a small black silhouette, upright, and took it for the trunk of a solitary tree. In any case I started toward it. It was a shepherd. Thirty sheep were lying about him on the baking earth.

He gave me a drink from his water-gourd and, a little later, took me to his cottage in a fold of the plain. He drew his water—excellent water—from a very deep natural well above which he had constructed a primitive winch.

The man spoke little. This is the way of those who live alone, but one felt that he was sure of himself, and confident in his assurance. That was unexpected in this barren country. He lived, not in a cabin, but in a real house built of stone that bore plain evidence of how his own efforts had reclaimed the ruin he had found there on his arrival. His roof was strong and sound. The wind on its tiles made the sound of the sea upon its shore.

The place was in order, the dishes washed, the floor swept, his rifle oiled; his soup was boiling over the fire. I noticed then that he was cleanly shaved, that all his buttons were firmly sewed on, that his clothing had been mended with the meticulous care

that makes the mending invisible. He shared his soup with me and afterwards, when I offered my tobacco pouch, he told me that he did not smoke. His dog, as silent as himself, was friendly without being servile.

It was understood from the first that I should spend the night there; the nearest village was still more than a day and a half away. And besides I was perfectly familiar with the nature of the rare villages in that region. There were four or five of them scattered well apart from each other on these mountain slopes, among white oak thickets, at the extreme end

of the wagon roads. They were inhabited by charcoalburners, and the living was bad. Families, crowd-
ed together in a climate that is excessively harsh both
in winter and in summer, found no escape from the
unceasing conflict of personalities. Irrational ambi-
tion reached inordinate proportions in the continual
desire for escape. The men took their wagonloads
of charcoal to the town, then returned. The soundest
characters broke under the perpetual grind. The
women nursed their grievances. There was rivalry in
everything, over the price of charcoal as over a pew
in the church, over warring virtues as over warring

vices as well as over the ceaseless combat between virtue and vice. And over all there was the wind, also ceaseless, to rasp upon the nerves. There were epidemics of suicide and frequent cases of insanity, usually homicidal.

The shepherd went to fetch a small sack and poured out a heap of acorns on the table. He began to inspect them, one by one, with great concentration, separating the good from the bad. I smoked my pipe. I did offer to help him. He told me that it was his job. And in fact, seeing the care he devoted to the task, I did not insist. That was the whole of our conversation. When he had set aside a large enough pile of good acorns he counted them out by tens, meanwhile eliminating the small ones or those which were slightly cracked, for now he examined them more closely. When he had thus selected one hundred perfect acorns he stopped and we went to bed.

There was peace in being with this man. The next day I asked if I might rest here for a day. He found

[15]

[16]

it quite natural—or, to be more exact, he gave me the impression that nothing could startle him. The rest was not absolutely necessary, but I was interested and wished to know more about him. He opened the pen and led his flock to pasture. Before leaving, he plunged his sack of carefully selected and counted acorns into a pail of water.

I noticed that he carried for a stick an iron rod as thick as my thumb and about a yard and a half long. Resting myself by walking, I followed a path parallel to his. His pasture was in a valley. He left the dog in charge of the little flock and climbed toward where I stood. I was afraid that he was about to rebuke me for my indiscretion, but it was not that at all: this was the way he was going, and he invited me to go along if I had nothing better to do. He climbed to the top of the ridge, about a hundred yards away.

There he began thrusting his iron rod into the earth, making a hole in which he planted an acorn; then he refilled the hole. He was planting oak trees. I asked him if the land belonged to him. He answered no. Did he know whose it was? He did not. He supposed it was community property, or perhaps belonged to people who cared nothing about it. He was not interested in finding out whose it was. He planted his hundred acorns with the greatest care.

After the midday meal he resumed his planting. I suppose I must have been fairly insistent in my questioning, for he answered me. For three years he had been planting trees in this wilderness. He had planted one hundred thousand. Of the hundred thousand, twenty thousand had sprouted. Of the twenty thousand he still expected to lose about half, to rodents or to the unpredictable designs of Providence. There remained ten thousand oak trees to grow where nothing had grown before.

That was when I began to wonder about the age of this man. He was obviously over fifty. Fifty-five, he told me. His name was Elzéard Bouffier. He had once had a farm in the lowlands. There he had had his life. He had lost his only son, then his wife. He had withdrawn into this solitude where his pleasure was to live leisurely with his lambs and his dog. It was his opinion that this land was dying for want of trees. He added that, having no very pressing busi-

ness of his own, he had resolved to remedy this state of affairs.

Since I was at that time, in spite of my youth, leading a solitary life, I understood how to deal gently with solitary spirits. But my very youth forced me to consider the future in relation to myself and to a certain quest for happiness. I told him that in thirty years his ten thousand oaks would be magnificent. He answered quite simply that if God granted him life, in thirty years he would have planted so many more that these ten thousand would be like a drop of water in the ocean.

Besides, he was now studying the reproduction of beech trees and had a nursery of seedlings grown from beechnuts near his cottage. The seedlings, which he had protected from his sheep with a wire fence, were very beautiful. He was also considering birches for the valleys where, he told me, there was a certain amount of moisture a few yards below the surface of the soil.

The next day, we parted.

THE following year came the War of 1914, in which I was involved for the next five years. An infantryman hardly had time for reflecting upon trees. To tell the truth, the thing itself had made no impression upon me; I had considered it as a hobby, a stamp collection, and forgotten it.

The war over, I found myself possessed of a tiny demobilization bonus and a huge desire to breathe fresh air for a while. It was with no other objective that I again took the road to the barren lands.

The countryside had not changed. However, beyond the deserted village I glimpsed in the distance a sort of greyish mist that covered the mountaintops like a carpet. Since the day before, I had begun to think again of the shepherd tree-planter. "Ten thousand oaks," I reflected, "really take up quite a bit of space."

I had seen too many men die during those five years not to imagine easily that Elzéard Bouffier was dead, especially since, at twenty, one regards men of fifty as old men with nothing left to do but die.

He was not dead. As a matter of fact, he was extremely spry. He had changed jobs. Now he had only four sheep but, instead, a hundred beehives. He had got rid of the sheep because they threatened his young trees. For, he told me (and I saw for myself), the war had disturbed him not at all. He had imperturbably continued to plant.

The oaks of 1910 were then ten years old and taller than either of us. It was an impressive spectacle. I was literally speechless and, as he did not talk, we spent the whole day walking in silence

through his forest. In three sections, it measured eleven kilometers in length and three kilometers at its greatest width. When you remembered that all this had sprung from the hands and the soul of this one man, without technical resources, you understood that men could be as effectual as God in other realms than that of destruction.

He had pursued his plan, and beech trees as high as my shoulder, spreading out as far as the eye could reach, confirmed it. He showed me handsome clumps of birch planted five years before—that is, in 1915, when I had been fighting at Verdun. He had set them out in all the valleys where he had guessed—and rightly—that there was moisture almost at the surface of the ground. They were as delicate as young girls, and very well established.

Creation seemed to come about in a sort of chain reaction. He did not worry about it; he was determinedly pursuing his task in all its simplicity; but as we went back toward the village I saw water flowing in brooks that had been dry since the memory of man. This was the most impressive result of chain reaction that I had seen. These dry streams had once, long ago, run with water. Some of the dreary villages

I mentioned before had been built on the sites of ancient Roman settlements, traces of which still remained; and archæologists, exploring there, had found fishhooks where, in the twentieth century, cisterns were needed to assure a small supply of water.

The wind, too, scattered seeds. As the water reappeared, so there reappeared willows, rushes, meadows, gardens, flowers, and a certain purpose in being alive. But the transformation took place so gradually that it became part of the pattern without causing any astonishment. Hunters, climbing into the wilderness in pursuit of hares or wild boar, had of course noticed the sudden growth of little trees, but had attributed it to some natural caprice of the earth. That is why no one meddled with Elzéard Bouffier's work. If he had been detected he would have had opposition. He was indetectable. Who in the villages or in the administration could have dreamed of such perseverance in a magnificent generosity?

To have anything like a precise idea of this exceptional character one must not forget that he worked in total solitude: so total that, toward the end of his life, he lost the habit of speech. Or perhaps it was that he saw no need for it.

IN 1933 he received a visit from a forest ranger
who notified him of an order against lighting fires
out of doors for fear of endangering the growth of
this *natural* forest. It was the first time, the man told
him naively, that he had ever heard of a forest grow-
ing of its own accord. At that time Bouffier was
about to plant beeches at a spot some twelve kilometers from his cottage. In order to avoid travel-
ling back and forth—for he was then seventy-five—
he planned to build a stone cabin right at the plan-
tation. The next year he did so.

In 1935 a whole delegation came from the Government to examine the "natural forest." There was a high official from the Forest Service, a deputy, technicians. There was a great deal of ineffectual talk. It was decided that something must be done and, fortunately, nothing was done except the only helpful thing: the whole forest was placed under the protection of the State, and charcoal burning prohibited. For it was impossible not to be captivated by the beauty of those young trees in the fulness of health, and they cast their spell over the deputy himself.

A friend of mine was among the forestry officers of the delegation. To him I explained the mystery. One day the following week we went together to see Elzéard Bouffier. We found him hard at work, some ten kilometers from the spot where the inspection had taken place.

This forester was not my friend for nothing. He was aware of values. He knew how to keep silent. I delivered the eggs I had brought as a present. We shared our lunch among the three of us and spent several hours in wordless contemplation of the countryside.

In the direction from which we had come the slopes were covered with trees twenty to twenty-five feet tall. I remembered how the land had looked in 1913: a desert . . . . Peaceful, regular toil, the vigorous mountain air, frugality and, above all, serenity of spirit had endowed this old man with awe-inspiring health. He was one of God's athletes. I wondered how many more acres he was going to cover with trees.

Before leaving, my friend simply made a brief suggestion about certain species of trees that the soil here seemed particularly suited for. He did not force the point. "For the very good reason," he told me later, "that Bouffier knows more about it than I do." At the end of an hour's walking—having turned it over in his mind—he added, "He knows a lot more about it than anybody. He's discovered a wonderful way to be happy!"

It was thanks to this officer that not only the forest but also the happiness of the man was protected. He delegated three rangers to the task, and so terrorized them that they remained proof against all the bottles of wine the charcoalburners could offer.

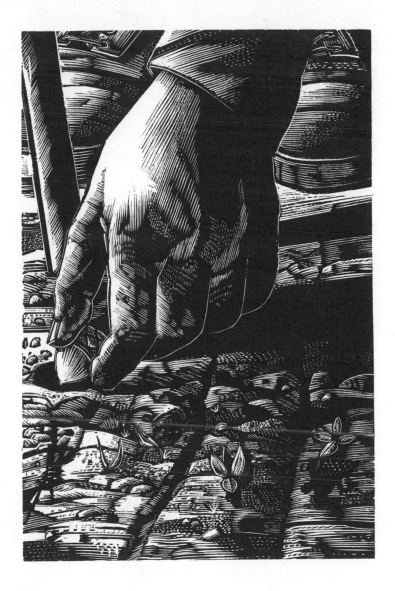

[31]

The only serious danger to the work occurred during the war of 1939. As cars were being run on gazogenes (wood-burning generators), there was never enough wood. Cutting was started among the oaks of 1910, but the area was so far from any railroads that the enterprise turned out to be financially unsound. It was abandoned. The shepherd had seen nothing of it. He was thirty kilometers away, peacefully continuing his work, ignoring the war of '39 as he had ignored that of '14.

I SAW Elzéard Bouffier for the last time in June of 1945. He was then eighty-seven. I had started back along the route through the wastelands; but now, in spite of the disorder in which the war had left the country, there was a bus running between the Durance Valley and the mountain. I attributed the fact that I no longer recognized the scenes of my earlier journeys to this relatively speedy transportation. It seemed to me, too, that the route took me through new territory. It took the name of a village to convince me that I was actually in that region that had been all ruins and desolation.

The bus put me down at Vergons. In 1913 this hamlet of ten or twelve houses had three inhabitants. They had been savage creatures, hating one another, living by trapping game, little removed, both physically and morally, from the conditions of prehistoric man. All about them nettles were feeding upon the remains of abandoned houses. Their condition had been beyond hope. For them, nothing but to await death—a situation which rarely predisposes to virtue.

Everything was changed. Even the air. Instead of the harsh dry winds that used to attack me, a gentle breeze was blowing, laden with scents. A sound like water came from the mountains: it was the wind in the forest. Most amazing of all, I heard the actual sound of water falling into a pool. I saw that a fountain had been built, that it flowed freely and—what touched me most—that someone had planted a linden beside it, a linden that must have been four years old, already in full leaf, the incontestable symbol of resurrection.

Besides, Vergons bore evidence of labor at the sort of undertaking for which hope is required. Hope, then, had returned. Ruins had been cleared away,

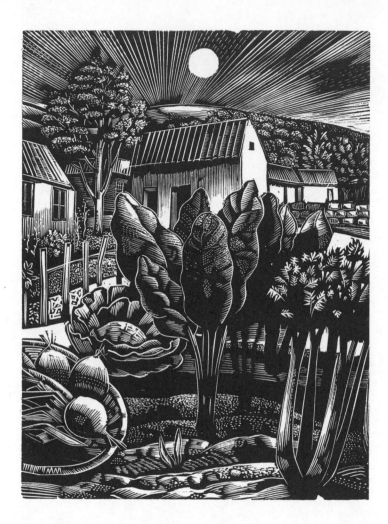

[36]

dilapidated walls torn down and five houses restored. Now there were twenty-eight inhabitants, four of them young married couples. The new houses, freshly plastered, were surrounded by gardens where vegetables and flowers grew in orderly confusion, cabbages and roses, leeks and snapdragons, celery and anemones. It was now a village where one would like to live.

From that point on I went on foot. The war just finished had not yet allowed the full blooming of life, but Lazarus was out of the tomb. On the lower slopes of the mountain I saw little fields of barley and of rye; deep in the narrow valleys the meadows were turning green.

It has taken only the eight years since then for the whole countryside to glow with health and prosperity. On the site of ruins I had seen in 1913 now stand neat farms, cleanly plastered, testifying to a happy and comfortable life. The old streams, fed by the rains and snows that the forest conserves, are flowing again. Their waters have been channeled. On each farm, in groves of maples, fountain pools over-

flow on to carpets of fresh mint. Little by little the villages have been rebuilt. People from the plains, where land is costly, have settled here, bringing youth, motion, the spirit of adventure. Along the roads you meet hearty men and women, boys and girls who understand laughter and have recovered a taste for picnics. Counting the former population, unrecognizable now that they live in comfort, more than ten thousand people owe their happiness to Elzéard Bouffier.

When I reflect that one man, armed only with his

own physical and moral resources, was able to cause this land of Canaan to spring from the wasteland, I am convinced that in spite of everything, humanity is admirable. But when I compute the unfailing greatness of spirit and the tenacity of benevolence that it must have taken to achieve this result, I am taken with an immense respect for that old and un-learned peasant who was able to complete a work worthy of God.

Elzéard Bouffier died peacefully in 1947 at the hospice in Banon.

AFTERWORD

I mustered enough courage to call upon Jean Giono in Manosque, Provence, at 11:00 A.M., August 15, 1970. His older daughter, Aline Giono, down from Paris for a few days, ushered me into the garden of their hillside home. Then dying from heart disease, Giono sat at a table, unable to walk any more, he told me at once. I could not believe his cultured voice, for I knew that he was self-taught. I have never recovered from the sight of him. He was positively stunning: slender, silver-haired, elegant, with delicate features, rosy cheeks, hooded blue eyes, casually dressed in tan slacks and mauve shirt. Without any hesitation he rushed into a dazzling discussion with me about books, critics, authors, Provence, his home, his life, his creativity. He begged me to stay and made me promise to return. I left that first day loaded down with gifts of his unpublished and privately published works, which I sent immediately to Butler Library, Columbia University. Less than two months later, Jean Giono died, midway through his seventy-fifth year.

Giono lived virtually his entire life in the little city of Manosque. His elderly father was a cobbler and his mother, he tells us in his early novel *Jean le bleu* (*Blue Boy*), ran a hand laundry. This family of three resided in the poorest of tenements where the child had only a blue view down into the well, or courtyard. At age sixteen, becoming sole support of the family, Giono left school and went to clerk in a bank. Eighteen years later, in 1929, he published his first two novels, *Colline* (*Hill of Destiny*) and *Un de Baumugnes* (*Lovers Are Never Losers*), both rave successes, in part thanks to the instant sponsorship of André Gide.

Years afterward Giono recalled the turning point in his life, that moment in the afternoon of December 20, 1911, when he could spare enough pennies to purchase the cheapest book he could find. It turned out to be a copy of Virgil's poems. He never forgot that first flush of his own creative energy: "My heart soared."

Giono laughingly said people in Paris sent him questionnaires because they did not want to read his books. But if we look at one of these documents he answered, we can hear him speak in his usual teasing voice and mood: My ideal of happiness? *Peace.* My favorite fictional hero? *Don Quixote.* My favorite historical character? *Machiavelli.* My heroines in real life? *There are no heroines in real life.* My painter? *Goya.* My musician? *Mozart.* My poet? *Villon. Baudelaire.* My color? *Red.* My flower? *The narcissus.* My chief character trait? *Generosity. Faithfulness.* My chief fault? *The generous lie.* What I want to be? *Lenient.* My preferred occupation? *Writing.*

* * *

Knowing his unique, exceptional, and, in fact, idiosyncratic patterns of thought, I am not surprised that Giono ran into difficulties with the American editors who in 1953 asked him to write a few pages about an unforgettable character. Apparently the publishers required a story about an actual unforgettable character, while Giono chose to write some pages about that character which to him *would be* most unforgettable. When what he wrote met with the objection that no "Bouffier" had died in the shelter at Banon, a tiny mountain hamlet, Giono donated his pages to all and sundry. Not long after the story was rejected, it was accepted by *Vogue* and published in March 1954 as "The Man Who Planted Hope and Grew Happiness." Giono later wrote an American admirer of the tale that his purpose in creating Bouffier "was to make people love the tree, or more precisely, to make them *love planting trees.*" Within a few years the story of Elzéard Bouffier swept around the world and was translated into at least a dozen languages. It has long since inspired reforestation efforts, worldwide.

We see from the opening sentence of the story how Giono interpreted the word "character," an individuality unforgettable if unselfish, generous beyond

[45]

measure, leaving on earth its mark without thought of reward. Giono believed he left his mark on earth when he wrote Elzéard Bouffier's story because he gave it away for the good of others, heedless of payment: "It is one of my stories of which I am the proudest. It does not bring me in one single penny and that is why it has accomplished what it was written for."

In *The Man Who Planted Trees,* the author's adventure commenced in June 1913, during a walking tour through Julius Caesar's ancient Roman province, still so called: Provence. As Giono trudged along the wild, deserted high plateau, he heard the wind growl like a lion over the ruins which lay like black carcasses and rush like ocean waves over the high country. Fearful and exposed, he saw mirages like the gaunt, black silhouette of a grieving woman he mistook for a dead tree. He met a shepherd, a *pastor* ministering to sheep, one of those solitary men associated from all time with congregations and Providence. By the end of World War I this same shepherd had become a beekeeper who already resembled God more narrowly by his power to create a new earth. He was planting oaks, beeches, and birches. Miraculously, water was conserved, dry stream beds filled again, and seeds germinated into gardens, meadows, and flowers. In 1933 this planter of trees of seventy-five years of age was clearly one of God's athletes. After World War II the author saw new villages in Canaan, where in 1913 all had lain waste. The shepherd had performed his solitary work, which Giono hoped he also had done. Both hoped to be worthy of God.

The name Elzéard calls to mind some forgotten Hebrew prophet, wise man, or Oriental king. The last name means in both French and English something grandiose: *bouffi, bouffé*, that is, puffed up (like a great man), puffed out (like wind, or a cloud in the sky). Such an old hero appears remarkably in most of Giono's early fiction, often a shepherd, or else some venerable alcoholic, storyteller, old hired man, or knife sharpener, but usually escorted by beasts: sheep, bees, a bull, a stag, a toad, or a serpent. Such lonely old men in their delirium directly hear the voice of God, or that of some ageless Greek divinity such as the great Pan. One must think of these variously gifted old men as embodying the creative gods themselves, as native survivals in this ancient Provence to which they continuously brought their wisdom, their knowledge of agriculture, their message of life indestructible, all of them teaching, like the titanic Dionysus, the precious secret of humanity's ancient kinship with the earth.

From the 1920s Giono continually praised this harmony whereby human beings conserved and enriched the earth where they coexisted with animals, both enriched by the silent but responsive, living vegetable kingdom. Giono also praised work done in solitude, where creation originates and, especially in humankind, where the free expression of compassion and pity begins.

When we express pity, Giono used to say, as for a living river cut off by dams, or pity for the helpless, suffering beast killed by cruel humankind, then we ourselves resemble the ancient yellow gods who still look down on us from Olympus. Should we not extend our compassion to the forest before it is felled by the woodcutters? This was not original in French literature, of course, but could have come to the child Giono as he read the *Fables* of La Fontaine in school. His thinking was reinforced by his favorite American "apostles of Nature," Walt Whitman and Henry David Thoreau.

We are probably accustomed to regional authors who express their love for animals and who encourage us to treat them with kindness and respect. Giono aside, we are less used to those writers who look upon the plant kingdom as coequal with the animal kingdom. We have begun to recognize a new fellowship with the silent vegetable world, because it purifies and renews the earth about us, because it comforts us, and because it reconciles us to death.

In *Solitude de la pitié* (1932) Giono illustrates all of this by telling us a whole series of tragi-comical stories. Once upon a time there was, he tells us, a feeble old country fellow named Jofroi, who sold his peach orchard to his neighbor Fonse in order to purchase an annuity for himself and his flustered old wife Barbe. Fine, until the day Fonse decided that the peach trees were diseased and old, and furthermore decided to cut them down. Then, in utter despair, Jofroi set about attempting to take his own life, but was always frustrated by Barbe. Jofroi never could stop explaining to anyone who would listen that these were his own trees, which he had planted, and watered by hand, and still owned. And owned forever.

In another tale from this collection, a tale I think of in English as "In the Woodcutters' Country," Giono tells how a young shepherd one day came to call on his friend Firmin, way up in the isolated hill country. The two friends finally could not stand to hear Firmin's wife crying in labor. So they walked all the way down into the valley, uprooted a large cypress, and lugged it back up the hills to home.

They planted it by the front door where Madelon could hear it singing to the wind. Her baby was christened in its shade. The tree burbled in the dry wind storms like a stream of water in heaven. Firmin passed on. Madelon too. The boy never came back from war. The tree is still there.

In his wonderful story of Elzéard Bouffier, Giono frankly seems to have intended to inspire a reforestation program that would renew the whole earth. His history of this imaginary shepherd, which is a compliment to Americans because of its relationship to the real Johnny Appleseed, calmly veers away from past and present time toward the future of newer and better generations. Giono termed his confidence in the future *espérance*, or hopefulness, not *espoir*, which is the masculine word for hope, but *espérance*, the feminine word designating the permanent state or condition of living one's life in hopeful tranquility. Whence springs this well of *espérance*, Giono wondered?

Hopefulness must spring, he decided, from literature and the profession of poetry. Authors only write. So, to be fair about it, they have an obligation to profess hopefulness, in return for their right to live and write. The poet must know the magical effect of certain words: hay, grass, meadows, willows, rivers, firs, mountains, hills. People have suffered so long inside walls that they have forgotten to be free, Giono thought. Human beings were not created to live forever in subways and tenements, for their feet long to stride through tall grass, or slide through running water. The poet's mission is to remind us of beauty, of trees swaying in the breeze, or pines groaning under snow in the mountain passes, of wild white horses galloping across the surf.

You know, Giono said to me, there are also times in life when a person has to rush off in pursuit of hopefulness.

* * *

During his lifetime Jean Giono, who considered himself to be Italian and Provençal, in addition to French, was judged one of the greatest writers of our age by such authorities as Henri Peyre and André Malraux. Both Peyre and Malraux ranked Giono first or second in French twentieth century literature: Giono, Montherlant, and Malraux (who included himself). Longevity counts most for an author, and Giono's works are still being edited and published after fifty-six years. Giono wrote over thirty novels, numerous essays, scores of stories, many of which were published as collections, plays, and film scripts. In 1953 he was awarded the Prix Monégasque for his collective work, and in 1954 he was elected to the Académie Goncourt, whose ten members award the annual Prix Goncourt.

In recent years some of Giono's most highly regarded novels have been reprinted by North Point Press and are once again available to English-speaking readers. These are: *Harvest* (1930), *Blue Boy* (1932), *Song of the World* (1934), *Joy of Man's Desiring* (1935), *Horseman on the Roof* (1951), and *The Straw Man* (1958).

Norma L. Goodrich
Claremont, California
May 1985

Norma L. Goodrich, a native Vermonter, has spent many years in France and is intimately familiar with Provence. After heading a private school in France during the 1950s, she returned to the United States and earned a Ph.D. in French literature at Columbia University. For the last twenty years she has lived in California and is presently Professor Emeritus of French and Comparative Literature at the Claremont Colleges. She is author of numerous scholarly works, including *Giono: Master of Fictional Modes*.

Chelsea Green is collaborating with Global ReLeaf to help promote a worldwide effort to plant trees.

Global ReLeaf
A Program of the American Forestry Association

The American Forestry Association (AFA), the oldest citizen's conservation organization in the U.S., is committed to helping ease the threat of global warming by planting trees. In 1989, the nonprofit group launched Global ReLeaf, a public education program designed to increase awareness of positive steps people can take to help the environment.

Global ReLeaf challenges people everywhere — from individual citizens to national leaders in government and business — to take positive action in reaching these goals:

- Expand the area of forests in both community and rural settings

- Reduce deforestation everywhere, particularly in the tropics, where the problem is most serious

- Assure that all forests are maintained in as healthy and productive condition as possible

- Advocate strong community forestry programs to reduce energy demand, increase cooling, and cut air pollution

- Reduce dependence on fossil fuels and control pollution from the fuels we use

- Enact effective legislation and research technologies to address these issues

For more information, call Global ReLeaf at 1-900-420-4545. The cost of the call is $5.00. Your call pays for planting a tree and supports Global ReLeaf action around the country. We'll also rush you detailed information on Global ReLeaf and how you can become further involved.

A program of
The American Forestry Association
P.O. Box 2000
Washington, DC 20013

COLOPHON

The Man Who Planted Trees
was designed, set in Times Roman, and illustrated
by Michael McCurdy.

It was printed by Bookcrafters
on Miami Book Antique, a recycled
and acid-free paper.

***

Michael McCurdy
is one of America's outstanding wood
engravers. He has designed and illustrated many books for both
adults and children, including the John Muir Library Series for
Sierra Club Books and *Hannah's Farm,*
a children's book he also authored.
The artist lives in
Great Barrington, Massachusetts.